The Moon Clipper, the most beautiful craft of the Golden Age, home to the young Man in the Moon and his guardian, Nightlight

Nightlight

The Family

JACK FROST

BY WILLIAM JOYCE

ILLUSTRATED BY

WILLIAM JOYCE AND

ANDREW THEOPHILOPOULOS

 Atheneum Books for Young Readers • New York London Toronto Sydney New Delhi

OF COURSE YOU KNOW THE GUARDIANS OF CHILDHOOD.

You've known them since before you can remember, and you'll know them till your memories are like twilight. The Man in the Moon brought the Guardians together. Santa, the Sandman, the Easter Bunny, the Tooth Fairy, and Mother Goose. They help watch over the children of Earth. But there is only one Guardian who is a child himself. And this is his story.

There was once a remarkable boy who never grew up. A boy who had two lives, and so he had two names. We know him as Jack Frost. But once upon a time, during the Golden Age, he was called Nightlight. He was a creature of light, with a bright uniform, and he glowed with courage and kindness. His very best friend was the Man in the Moon, back when the Man in the Moon himself was just a very little boy. It was Nightlight's duty to light his friend's way.

Like the truest friend, Nightlight could feel when the little Man in the Moon was happy or sad or afraid. He'd promised the baby's parents that he'd protect him and had even taken this oath:

> *"Watch over our child. Guide him safely from the ways*
> *of harm.*
> *Keep happy his heart, brave his soul, rosy his cheeks.*
> *Guard with your life his hopes and dreams,*
> *For he is all that we have, all that we are,*
> *And all that we will ever be."*

But Pitch, the Nightmare King, hoped to take the Man in the Moon and make him his darkling prince.

Nightlight could feel his friend's fear as Pitch pursued them. He would never let the Nightmare King harm the boy.

After a fierce and valiant battle, Nightlight saved
the young Man in the Moon from Pitch.

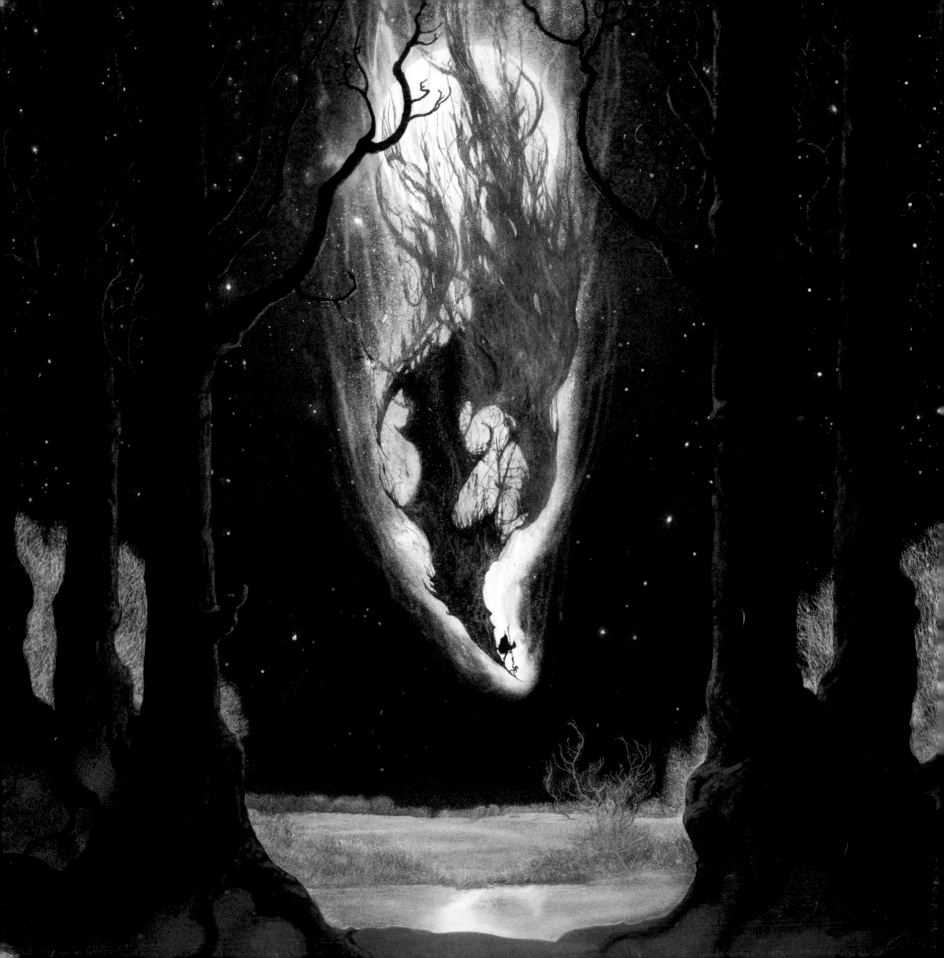

He brought Pitch and his *Nightmare Galleon* down, but this victory came with a heavy price.

Nighlight could feel the little Man in the Moon was safe and unafraid, which gave him comfort. His bright uniform fell away, and for days and nights unending, he drifted, until all he knew of his life, and what had been his name, became lost. He was a boy forever frozen in time.

hen one night he felt a light above him, and he once again opened his eyes. When he emerged, he was no longer a creature of the Golden Age, but an icy boy of Earth whose slightest breath or touch brought spirals of frost. And though the Man in the Moon was now grown up, he never forgot his best friend's courage and kindness. The Man in the Moon kept watch.

He kept watch as the boy sailed on icy winds, going
around Earth from night to day and back again
in less time than it takes to sing a lullaby.

He kept watch as the boy rode among the clouds while birds of every kind flew through the icy air with him. The rain, the wind, the clouds, and the creatures of the air and forest loved the boy, for he was as wild and free as they were.

But the boy was lonely, and his heart ached for something he could not quite remember. Always cold, he longed for warmth. And as his longings grew, his coldness began to sweep down. The forest changed color, and the leaves turned to snowflakes.

The snow then came in great storms till all the world grew white. And so his name became Jackson Overland Frost.

But the Man in the Moon, ever watchful, shined down and helped Jack Frost see what would soothe his cold and stormy heart and make him remember.

As if carried by the light
of the Moon, memories of courage
and kindness surrounded Jack and
guided him on . . .

. . . and he remembered his oath.

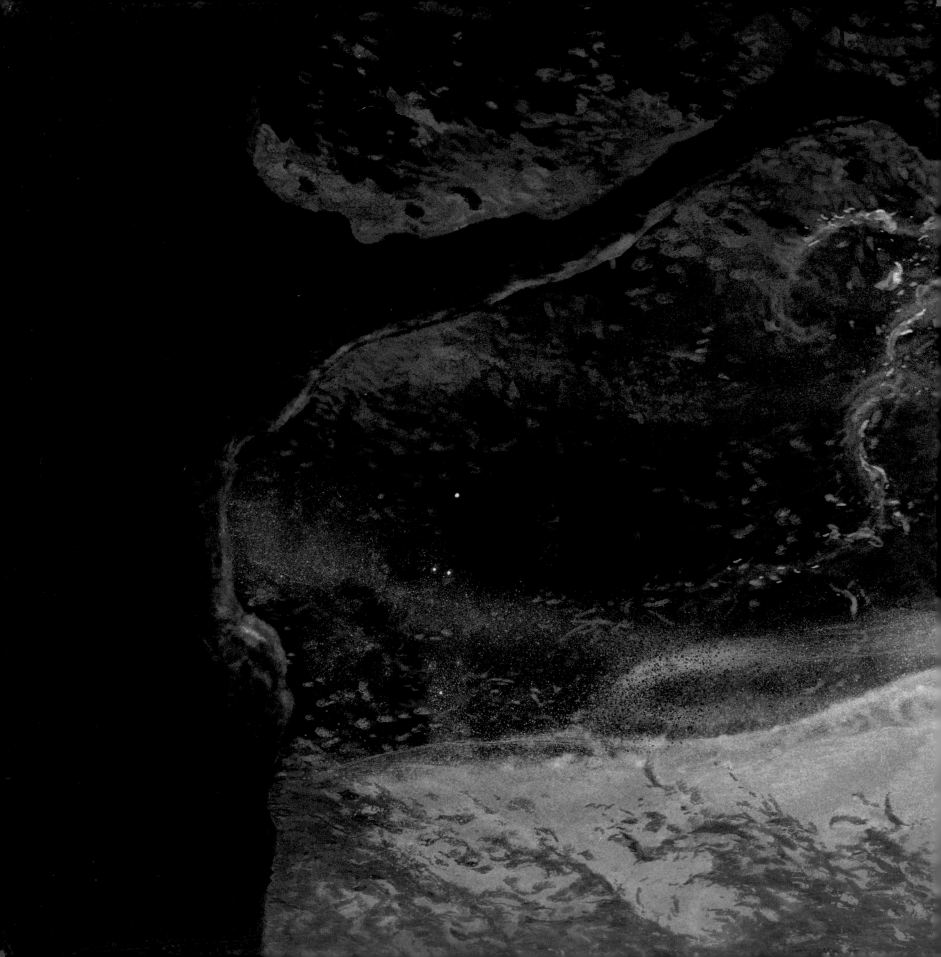

And as his lonely heart changed, so did the oath:

I will watch over the children of Earth,
Guide them safely from ways of harm,

Keep happy their hearts, brave their souls, and rosy their cheeks.
I will guard with my life their hopes and dreams,

For they are all that I have, all that I am,
And all that I will ever be.

And his heart ached no more.

You can hear Jack's oath in the song of a bird or the falling of a leaf or the changing of the seasons. Like the stars and the Moon . . .

. . . Jack Frost will always be there.

Jack Frost